THIS
BOOK
BELONGS
TO

_____

_____

_____

DATE

THE BOOKS ABOUT ADDY

❋

MEET ADDY · An American Girl

Addy and her mother try to escape from slavery because they hope to be free and to reunite their family.

❋

ADDY LEARNS A LESSON · A School Story

Addy starts her life as a free person in Philadelphia. She learns about reading and writing for the first time—and about the real meaning of freedom.

❋

ADDY'S SURPRISE · A Christmas Story

During the holiday season, Addy and Momma are generous with the little money they've saved—and thrilled by a great surprise.

ADDY'S
SURPRISE
A CHRISTMAS STORY
BY CONNIE PORTER

ILLUSTRATIONS MELODYE ROSALES

VIGNETTES RENÉE GRAEF. IANE S. VARDA

PLEASANT COMPANY

Published by Pleasant Company Publications Incorporated
© Copyright 1993 by Pleasant Company Incorporated
All rights reserved. No part of this book may be used or reproduced in
any manner whatsoever without written permission except in the case of
brief quotations embodied in critical articles and reviews.
For information, address: Book Editor,
Pleasant Company Publications Incorporated,
8400 Fairway Place, P.O. Box 620998,
Middleton, WI 53562.

First Edition.
Printed in the United States of America.
93 94 95 96 97 98 RRD 10 9 8 7 6 5 4 3 2 1

The American Girls Collection® is a registered trademark of
Pleasant Company Incorporated.

PICTURE CREDITS
The following individuals and organizations have generously given permission to reprint
illustrations contained in "Looking Back": pp. 60–61—U.S. Army Military History Institute
(mess hall, children); Abby Aldrich Rockefeller Folk Art Center (toy); Hargrett Rare Book and
Manuscript Library/University of Georgia Libraries (recipe book); pp. 62–63—Moorland-
Spingarn Research Center, Howard University (Charlotte Forten); The William Gladstone
Collection, Westport, Connecticut (family photos); National Archives (soldiers around fire);
Right and Left, 1850, The Museums at Stony Brook, Stony Brook, Long Island (fiddle player);
pp. 64–65—The Granger Collection, New York (emancipation proclamation);
McLellan Lincoln Collection, John Hay Library, Brown University, Photo by John Miller
(Lincoln portrait).

Edited by Roberta Johnson
Designed by Myland McRevey and Jane S. Varda
Art Directed by Kathleen A. Brown

Library of Congress Cataloging-in-Publication Data

Porter, Connie Rose, 1959–
Addy's surprise : a christmas story / by Connie Porter ; illustrations, Melodye Rosales ;
vignettes, Renée Graef and Jane S. Varda. — 1st ed.
p. cm. — (The American girls collection)
Summary: Addy and her mother forego their Christmas plans to help the newly freed slaves
arriving in Philadelphia during the Civil War.

ISBN 1-56247-080-9 — ISBN 1-56247-079-5 (pbk.)
[1. Christmas—Fiction. 2. Mothers and daughters—Fiction.
3. Afro-Americans—Fiction.]
I. Rosales, Melodye, ill. II. Title. III. Series.
PZ7.P825Ae   1993   [Fic]—dc20   93-5162   CIP   AC

FOR MY NIECE, TIA PORTER

TABLE OF CONTENTS

ADDY'S FAMILY
AND FRIENDS

ADDY'S FAMILY

POPPA
Addy's father, whose dream gives the family strength.

MOMMA
Addy's mother, whose love helps the family survive.

ADDY
A courageous girl, smart and strong, growing up during the Civil War.

SAM
Addy's fifteen-year-old brother, determined to be free.

ESTHER
Addy's one-year-old sister.

SARAH MOORE
*Addy's good friend, who
helps Addy learn about
freedom and friendship.*

MRS. FORD
*The firm-but-fair
owner of the dress shop
where Momma works.*

REVEREND DRAKE
*The inspiring minister at
Trinity A.M.E. Church.*

MR. DELMONTE
*The owner of a
secondhand shop in
Addy's neighborhood.*

WINDS OF WINTER

Addy Walker knew that winter had come to Philadelphia even before she opened her eyes. An icy wind whistled through the crack in the garret window. Momma had just gotten up, letting a puff of cold air in the bed when she lifted the heavy quilt. But her place was still warm, so Addy snuggled into it.

Momma's gentle voice called to her. "Addy, honey, I need your help over here. Snow's coming right in through the window."

Addy peeked out from under the quilt. In the dim gray light of morning, she saw Momma straining to close the window. Its panes were white with frost. A little pile of snow had built up on the

1

window sill, and more snow had blown across the floor. "I'm coming, Momma," she said.

Addy crawled out of bed and shivered over to the window to help Momma. Together, they pulled down on the window, struggling to close it. But the window wouldn't budge.

"Go get them rags next to the stove," Momma said.

Addy got the rags and returned to Momma.

"Help me stuff these in the crack, Addy," said Momma, as she poked the rags between the window and the sill. "Stuff them good. They all we got to keep the wind from coming in."

Addy put one cold foot on top of the other to try to warm up her feet. "Can't we light the stove this morning, Momma?" she asked. "It's so cold in here."

"No, honey," Momma said. "We got just enough coal to last us the week if we use it only for cooking supper." She smiled at Addy and gave her a quick, warm hug. "Now you wash up and get ready for school. And hustle, you hear? Then you won't feel the cold so bad."

Addy splashed icy cold water from the basin

over her face and dressed quickly, dancing around in her stocking feet. She waited to pull on her boots until the very end. They were still wet from the puddle she had stepped in on her way home from school yesterday. Though she had set them by the stove last night, the fire hadn't been warm long enough to dry them out.

Addy wrapped her shawl around her shoulders and sat down at the table to eat the cornbread Momma had set out for her. She crumbled it in a bowl and poured buttermilk over it. As she ate, she spied a pile of fabric folded neatly on Momma's chair, with a spool of thread and a pair of scissors on top.

"You was up late again sewing, Momma, wasn't you?" asked Addy.

"I got to finish this dress for Mrs. Howell," answered Momma. "Mrs. Ford say Mrs. Howell is real particular."
Momma unfolded the fabric and squinted at one of the seams she had sewn last night. "It's hard to see my stitches by candlelight. We sure do need a lamp."

"How much we got saved for it?" asked Addy.

"Can I count up the money in the milk bottle again?"

Momma nodded. "Sure you can," she said, "but I ain't put nothing in since you counted it last week."

"I put my tips in last Saturday, Momma," Addy said proudly. "I got two big tips when I delivered them dresses to Society Hill for Mrs. Ford."

"That's good, Addy," said Momma. She reached into their hiding place behind the stove, picked up the milk bottle, and handed it to Addy.

Addy turned the bottle upside down and shook it so that the coins poured out. Then she carefully counted the pennies, half dimes, and dimes.

"We got one dollar and fifty-seven cents," announced Addy.

"Well, that ain't enough for a lamp," said Momma. "Guess we gonna have to wait a little longer. Just hope I don't have to pull them stitches out of one of them seams in that dress."

Addy finished her breakfast and washed her bowl and spoon in the bucket of water that stood by the stove. Then she sat back down so Momma could brush and braid her hair. She looked at the thick folds of green and red plaid taffeta that lay over the chair next to her.

"Them rich girls sure got pretty dresses," said Addy.

"Sure do," said Momma. "Isabella Howell's gonna wear that one to some fancy Christmas party."

"Remember last Christmas, Momma?" asked Addy. She thought back to last year when she and Momma were on the plantation with Poppa, her brother Sam, and baby sister Esther. "Master Stevens gave us a real skinny chicken. Sam wouldn't even eat it after you cooked it. He was mad because of how hard we worked. He said one chicken couldn't make up for a whole year of work. But I was hungry, and I ate it."

"I remember," Momma said, "but Sam ate my sweet-potato pudding. He liked that."

"And Poppa did, too," Addy said. "Sweet-potato pudding was Poppa's favorite. He always said so. He always . . ."

Addy stopped. She and Momma did not even know where Poppa and Sam were. And they had to

"It ain't gonna be just a dream, Momma. It's really gonna happen someday, ain't it?" Addy asked hopefully. "Ain't we all gonna be together someday?"

"Someday, honey. Someday. That dream keep me going. That and your bright face." Momma finished the second braid and leaned over to kiss the top of Addy's head.

☀

On the way to school that morning, Addy asked her friend Sarah what Christmas was like in freedom. Sarah described the celebration at church.

"I hope it's gonna be just like last year," said Sarah. "The altar was all decorated with pine branches. In the middle was a manger with baby Jesus, and Mary and Joseph kneeling next to it. There was three wise men and a bunch of angels and even a silvery star hanging from the ceiling. Lots of candles was on the altar. The whole church was glowing and beautiful. I'm telling you, Addy, it's the prettiest thing you'll ever see. Ever."

Addy could barely imagine something so lovely.

Sarah went on, "After the service, we go downstairs for the big Christmas dinner. Everybody bring something to share and everyone in the whole church sit down like one great big family."

"Momma said we was gonna bring sweet-potato pudding, just like we had last year for Christmas," said Addy.

"Mmm, that sound good," said Sarah brightly, "but I ain't told you the best part yet, Addy. After dinner, there's a special shadow play for children."

"What's that?" asked Addy.

"Well, it's kind of hard to describe," said Sarah.

"We sit in a dark room that has this big sheet hanging in the front. Behind it, there's this bright lamp. People in front of the lamp make shadows on the sheet. They act out the Christmas story while it's read out loud."

"I bet it's real nice," Addy said.

"You gonna love it," Sarah said excitedly. "And this year my momma's letting me sing in the children's choir. You should join, too. We practice every Saturday till Christmas."

"I wish I could, but I can't," said Addy. "Saturday is when I work for Mrs. Ford. I'm doing errands and deliveries so she and Momma can spend all their time sewing Christmas dresses for the customers. Mrs. Ford let me keep the tips from the deliveries. I had to promise I would keep up with my lessons."

"What are you going to do with your money?" asked Sarah.

"Momma and me saving for a lamp," answered Addy. "Maybe by the time I finish all the Christmas deliveries, we might have enough saved up."

"Well, don't worry, Addy," said Sarah kindly. "If you can't come to choir practice, I'll teach you the songs. Then you can sing on Christmas along with everyone else."

"I'd like that," said Addy. She smiled at her friend.

"We can start right now," said Sarah. "The first song we always sing is 'Joy to the World.' Here's how it goes." With that, Sarah began to sing. Addy listened and then hummed along. Soon she knew the words.

"Joy to the world!" the two girls sang together as they hurried through the winter streets to school.

SOMETHING PRETTY

Early on Saturday morning, Addy set out on her errands and deliveries for Mrs. Ford. She brought a bill to a customer on Society Hill. Then she went to the dry goods store a few blocks away to pick up supplies that Mrs. Ford had ordered. The thread, buttons, ribbon, and fringe were wrapped into one parcel before Addy left the store.

Addy held on to her parcel tightly as she stepped around the slush and dirty puddles in the streets. On the way to her next stop, she passed the windows of Mr. Delmonte's Secondhand Shop. Sometimes she and Momma went there to look for clothes or pots and pans. The socks Addy had on today had come from Mr. Delmonte's. There was a small darn in the heel of one sock, but the other was as good as new.

Addy stopped for a minute to look in the window. Lying among the used shoes, wool caps, and old belts was a bright patch of red cloth. It looked like the corner of a scarf, but most of it was hidden behind a rusty tea kettle. Addy went inside to take a closer look.

Mr. Delmonte recognized her right away. "Good morning, Addy," he said in his jolly way. "What brings you here today?"

"Can I see that red scarf in the window?" Addy asked.

Mr. Delmonte reached into the window display and moved the tea kettle so he could lift out the scarf and hand it to Addy. "It's a beauty," he said. "Hardly looks worn."

Addy unfolded the scarf. It was like new. The red fabric was soft and smooth. Addy held it up to her cheek. Right then she knew she wanted Momma to have the scarf. *Momma should have something pretty like this,* thought Addy. *She work so hard. She'd look so beautiful in this when we go to the Christmas service at*

"Momma should have something pretty like this," thought Addy.
"She work so hard."

14

church. Addy was almost afraid to ask about the price, but she looked up at Mr. Delmonte.

"How much it cost?" she asked.

"Twenty cents," answered Mr. Delmonte. "It's a good price for something that looks like it's never been worn."

Addy was discouraged. She didn't have 20 cents. But she had to buy that scarf somehow.

"Please, Mr. Delmonte," she said, "could you put it away for me? I'm gonna try my best to get the money to buy it."

"Well, I'll put it back behind that rusty kettle again," answered Mr. Delmonte. "You're the only person who's spotted it since I put it in the window last week. It'll probably stay there a little longer."

"I hope so," said Addy as she carefully folded the scarf and handed it back to Mr. Delmonte.

The feel of the soft material and its bright red color stayed in Addy's mind as she headed back to Mrs. Ford's shop. *How am I gonna get 20 cents?* she wondered.

Back at the shop, Mrs. Ford had three packages for her to deliver, all wrapped in brown paper. "These go to Society Hill," said Mrs. Ford as she handed them to Addy. "Be careful. Don't splash mud on them."

"Yes, ma'am," said Addy.

The streets were busier that afternoon than they were in the morning. Addy had to dodge around throngs of people bustling in and out of shops. Her packages were clumsy, and she worried about dropping them on the sloppy sidewalks. After Momma had worked so hard, Addy wanted to make sure the dresses were delivered in perfect condition.

The last delivery was on Spruce Street. As Addy walked toward the address, she saw an old man lighting the street lamps. The lamps cast a golden glow on the wet sidewalks. When Addy got to the house, she rang the bell and waited for the big door to open. A maid finally came, and Addy handed her the last bundle.

"This is from Mrs. Ford's shop," she said proudly.

The maid took the package and handed Addy five pennies. Addy thanked her and turned away. As she walked back down Spruce Street, she curled her fingers around the coins inside her mitten.

Suddenly, Addy had an idea. She decided to stop by Mr. Delmonte's shop again on the way home, just to be sure the soft red scarf was still there. As she approached the store, Mr. Delmonte was just locking up.

"Don't worry, Addy," he said. "The scarf is still here. I moved it off in the corner a bit, but you can see it if you know where to look."

The two of them stood at the window together. Mr. Delmonte headed down the street, but Addy stayed at the window, thinking about her idea. *If I put half my tips in the milk bottle,* she thought, *and keep the other half, maybe I can save enough money to buy the scarf for Momma!* Addy lingered a little longer, staring at the scarf in the fading light, thinking how pretty Momma would look in it. Then she headed back to Mrs. Ford's shop.

By the time she got to the shop, her feet were numb with cold and her nose felt frozen.

"You look frozen stiff, child," said Mrs. Ford, peering above her spectacles. Mrs. Ford had a tape measure draped around her neck. Momma had a ribbon thrown across one shoulder as she sewed fringe on the end of a sash. They looked busy, and

Addy knew she shouldn't bother them.

"Momma, can I light the stove upstairs now?" asked Addy. "Please?"

"No, Addy," Momma answered. "You know we don't light the stove until I start cooking supper. You head on upstairs. I'll be up as soon as I finish this sash. Then we'll light the stove."

"Yes, Momma," said Addy.

As she headed out the door, she heard Mrs. Ford ask Momma, "How is everything up in the garret?"

"Everything is fine," Momma answered quickly. "We get by."

Addy wanted to turn around and tell Mrs. Ford the truth, that it was freezing in the garret, and dark, and sometimes very lonely. On the plantation, Addy had been allowed to spend more time with Momma than she was here. She wanted to tell Mrs. Ford about the broken window and the snow on the floor. But Addy knew Momma would not want her to complain.

"We get by," Addy said softly to herself as she climbed the stairs.

When she got to the top, she lit the candle on the table. Addy turned her mitten upside down and let her tip money fall onto the table. She brought the milk bottle out from behind the stove and set it next to the money. Then Addy went over to the bed and lifted up a corner of the mattress. There she found the kerchief that she had brought from the plantation when she and Momma had escaped from slavery. Tied in one corner was the half dime Uncle Solomon had given her. It was the only money they had when they headed north for freedom. "Freedom's got a cost," Uncle Solomon had said when he gave it to Addy. She had saved it for something very special, something important.

Addy brought the kerchief over to the table and divided her tip money into two piles. She dropped one pile into the milk bottle and then carefully tied the other coins into the corner of her kerchief. With Uncle Solomon's half dime, she had ten cents in the kerchief. That was half of what she needed for Momma's red scarf. *I'm halfway there!* Addy thought to herself. The thought made her so happy, she didn't think about the cold.

CHAPTER
THREE

—

FREEDOM AIN'T
FREE

At church the next morning, Momma
and Addy sat side by side in the
women's section. Addy looked across
the aisle where all the men sat and imagined that
someday her poppa would be sitting over there,
smiling and giving her a wink that said, "You my
favorite girl."

When the deep notes of the organ sounded,
everyone stood to sing. The first song was one of
Addy's favorites. Auntie Lula had taught it to her
back on the plantation. Now Addy sang out with the
others in joy.

This little light of mine,
I'm gonna let it shine,
Let it shine, let it shine, let it shine.

After a long prayer, Reverend Drake began his sermon. "I want to begin this morning by reading from the book of Luke. Turn to chapter two, verses six and seven."

Momma took a Bible from the rack on the pew in front of them. Addy helped her find the passage.

Reverend Drake said, "This passage I'm about to read to you is about Mary and Joseph."

Addy and Momma and the other members followed along as Reverend Drake read: "And she brought forth her firstborn son, and wrapped him in swaddling clothes, and laid him in a manger; because there was no room for them in the inn.

"Now, this is the story of Christmas, the story of the birth of Jesus. The time had come for Mary to give birth to Jesus. Let me tell you people, time is a curious thing. It can't be stopped like a clock," Reverend Drake said.

"You right, Reverend," one church member called out.

"Time keeps right on moving. And I'm here to tell you the *time* for freedom has come for thousands of our people. These freedmen are waiting right now in Washington, D.C., and other cities. And they need our help. Stay with me, now," Reverend Drake preached. "Think with me. Because I'm here to tell you this morning, freedom ain't free!"

A church member shouted back, "You preaching the truth!"

Addy scooted over closer to Momma and laid her head on Momma's shoulder. Momma put her arm around Addy and rocked gently on the pew. Addy liked coming to church. Anyone who wanted to could take part in the service. If you felt like answering the reverend, you could. If you felt like crying, or laughing, or clapping to the music the choir sang, you could.

Reverend Drake continued, "Some of you already know what I'm talking about because there was a *time* when you came to freedom, and you found out what freedom was about. It wasn't free! You needed food to eat, clothes to wear, a place to stay."

"Amen!" Momma replied.

"You found out what freedom was about," Reverend Drake said.
"It wasn't free!"

"I'm here to tell you people, time ain't gonna stop for those thousands of freedmen who need our help. As I speak to you, babies are being born, and children are hungry, and mothers and fathers have no place to lay their heads at night. They need our help now, today!" Reverend Drake said, his voice getting louder.

Addy looked up at Momma and saw tears running down her face. Addy gave Momma a little hug.

"As we enter the season of Advent, the time of preparing for Christmas, let God work through you. When the collection boxes are passed this morning, remember to put in a little extra for our Freedmen's Fund. These people are your cousins, your brothers and sisters, your mothers and fathers," Reverend Drake said, pounding on the pulpit.

"It might mean you have to sacrifice. If you can't give of your money, give of your time. Next Saturday a group of freedmen are coming in at the pier. Come help us welcome them to freedom.

"I close by saying, freedom can be a lonely walk through the wilderness and dark. But you can make a difference between a lonely night and one filled with light and hope!"

On the way home from church, Momma and Addy walked hand in hand, humming "This Little Light of Mine." Even though it was cold out, Addy felt a warm glow inside.

"I been thinking about what Reverend Drake said this morning," said Momma slowly. "He made me remember how it was for you and me when we first came to Philadelphia. We had nothing. The church helped us when we needed it. Now we done saved more than a dollar fifty. The freedmen need our help right now. They need our savings more than we do. We can get along without a lamp, but they can't get along without help. What do you think?"

At first, Addy did not say anything. It was true. She and Momma could get along without the lamp. But they had saved so hard for it. A lamp would help her see better when she did her homework, and it would help Momma when she had to sew late at night. Addy could imagine how nice it would be to have a lamp when Sam and Poppa and Esther returned, when their family was at last together again. She could picture their faces glowing in the bright light as they gathered around the dinner table. But then she remembered how scared and lonely she and Momma had been when they first came to Philadelphia, and how the church had helped them find work, a place to live, and friends.

"I think we should give our money to the church," Addy said. "Other people helped us. The money might even help Sam or Poppa or Esther come to us."

"Even if it don't," replied Momma, "it's gonna help *somebody*. That's what's important." She squeezed Addy's hand. "We'll give the church our money next Sunday."

With a pang of guilt, Addy remembered the ten cents she had knotted up in her kerchief. Should she give that to help the freedmen, too? *No*, thought Addy. *I can't give that money away. It's for Momma's Christmas surprise.* Addy decided to keep the money. She was determined to buy the scarf and show Momma how much she loved her. She would find another way to help the freedmen. "Momma," she asked, "can I go to the pier next Saturday to help out with the freedmen?"

"I think that would be fine, Addy," said Momma, "just so you finish all of Mrs. Ford's deliveries."

"I will, Momma," Addy promised.

CHAPTER
FOUR

—

THE COST OF FREEDOM

When Addy arrived at the pier the next Saturday, Reverend Drake was already handing out old clothes and blankets to the people who had just gotten off the boat. Sarah and her mother were there, just as they had been when Addy and Momma arrived in Philadelphia last summer. Addy was glad to see them.

"What am I supposed to say to these folks?" Addy asked Sarah.

"You ain't got to say nothing special," Sarah said. "Just be yourself."

"I wish I could be like you," Addy said. "When you met us, you made me feel like I was coming home."

"I was scared the day I met you," Sarah admitted, "and look how good things turned out for us."

The pier was slick with mud. Garbage floated in the dark, icy water, and the newly freed people huddled together in silent groups. They looked cold, frightened, hungry, and lost. Addy closed her eyes for a second. *Esther. Sam. Poppa. Be here. Be here,* Addy wished. But when she opened her eyes, there were no familiar faces in the crowd. Addy's heart sank.

Just then she saw a thin woman who held a bundle in her arms. Addy heard a sharp cry. For a second, Addy thought it was Esther crying, and her heart started to pound. Then she saw a little hand reach up from the bundle. Quickly, Addy pulled her shawl from around her shoulders and handed it to the woman, who thanked her and wrapped the shawl around her baby.

Addy held out her arms. "I can carry the baby, if you like," she said. "I'll be careful."

The woman smiled weakly. "Thank you kindly," she said. She handed the baby to Addy. Addy cradled the baby in her arms just as she used to cradle Esther. The baby's eyes were bright as buttons. Addy held the baby close to her chest, hoping to warm her. The baby waved her arms and grabbed the cowrie shell necklace Addy wore around her neck. The baby's mother smiled. "She like you," she said. "She don't take a shine to just anybody."

The woman rode back to the church in the wagon that Reverend Drake had brought, along with an old man who was coughing so hard his whole body shook. Another man in the wagon had been limping along with a stick he used as a crutch. His foot was bandaged in dirty rags. Addy looked at the poor, tired people who plodded along behind the wagon. Some had no shoes. Others wore tattered clothes. Addy held the baby closer to her, trying to keep her warm.

"Where y'all from?" Addy asked the baby's mother.

"We coming up from Baltimore," said the woman. "All the slaves on our plantation was turned out about a month ago. We was told we was free and we had to get. But we ain't had nowhere to go. No food. No nothing. Me and some others

Addy held the baby close, hoping to warm her.

walked together. For a week, we ate almost nothing but grass. We walked until we got to Baltimore."

"Things gonna be better here," promised Addy. "The people at the church helped me and my momma. They'll help you, too."

When the wagon arrived back at church, Addy led the woman to Fellowship Hall in the basement. The big room was warm and dry and filled with the smell of delicious food. Many church members were there to help serve food to the freedmen. Addy remembered how happy she and Momma had been in this same place, eating their first warm meal in freedom on their first day in Philadelphia. She said good-bye to the woman. "You be safe now," she said. "People in the church gonna be your family." Addy hugged the baby one last time. Memories of Esther filled her mind, and she squeezed her eyes tight to stop the tears. Then Addy left to go to Mrs. Ford's.

Back at the shop, there were more errands to do and three deliveries to make. Addy hurried along the busy streets. She saw women in fancy hats and fur coats carrying packages wrapped in bright paper. Usually Addy would have been fascinated with their fine clothes and fancy manners, but today they seemed silly. She remembered the people shivering at the pier. A man in a top hat strolled by, swinging a fine walking stick. Addy thought of the man at the pier with his foot in dirty bandages. When Addy made a delivery to one of the biggest houses on Society Hill, all she could think of were the freedmen who had arrived that morning. None of them had a place to stay at all.

Addy got tips from the first two houses she went to. The coins jingled in her mitten, and she began to think cheerfully about the scarf that she would soon be able to buy for Momma. If she got a five-cent tip from her last delivery, she would have just enough for the scarf. Addy began to walk faster. Her last delivery was the beautiful plaid dress for Isabella Howell. It was the dress Momma had worked the hardest on, and Addy was very proud to be delivering it. She lifted the shiny brass knocker on the front door and banged it loudly three times.

Soon a woman came. "Who are you?" she asked coldly.

"I'm Addy Walker. This here is a dress from Mrs. Ford's dress shop. It's for Isabella Howell."

"Very well then," said the maid as she took the package. "Wait here."

Addy stood in the entrance of the Howells' mansion. The house looked more beautiful than any house she'd ever seen. A staircase of dark wood curved up to the second floor. Addy could see into the living room, too. She saw a high-backed pink couch and pink chairs. Instead of kerosene lamps, the room had gas lamps, each one lighted and covered by a glass globe. In the corner, a decorated Christmas tree reached up to the ceiling. The lamplight filled the room with a rosy glow, and a fire burned in the hearth.

The maid returned shortly and pressed a coin into Addy's hand. "Here's a tip for you, child. Now run along," she said, hurrying Addy out the door.

Addy was outside. The big door had closed behind her before she looked at the coin in her hand. She couldn't believe what she saw. "A dime!" said Addy out loud. "A whole dime." It was the biggest tip Addy had ever gotten. She slid it into her mitten. Now she had enough for Momma's scarf! She even had a little extra to put in the milk bottle to start saving for the lamp again.

Addy skipped down the walk and ran all the way back to the shop. She didn't even stop in to see Momma and Mrs. Ford. Instead, she ran upstairs and took her kerchief out from under the mattress. She untied the knot and let the coins fall on the table. She turned her mitten upside down and dumped the tips she had made that day into the pile of money. Carefully, she counted 20 cents for Momma's scarf. Then she dropped the rest of the money in the milk bottle. The 20 cents went into her mitten. She would get the scarf this afternoon after she finished her errands. She could hardly wait!

Addy's last chore of the day was to get Mrs. Ford's scissors sharpened. The sharpener's shop was not too far from Mr. Delmonte's shop. If Addy hurried, she could get the scissors sharpened and buy the scarf before it got dark.

The grinding wheel that sharpened the scissors made a loud, whining noise, so Addy waited outside. People pushed past her in a hurry to get home. Streetcars clanged and carriages rushed by, but she hardly noticed them. All she could think about was Momma's beautiful scarf and how surprised she would be on Christmas morning.

A woman pushing a fancy baby buggy wheeled toward Addy and stopped in front of the shop. The buggy was too big to fit through the door, so the woman parked it next to Addy and lifted out a little baby all bundled in soft fleecy blankets. The baby started to fuss. Suddenly, Addy remembered the baby she'd held that morning. Then she began to think about Esther. *My sister might not be as lucky as that baby at the pier. Who's gonna give money for her to come to freedom?*

Addy felt the coins she held in her hand inside the mitten. It was only 20 cents. But if everyone gave as much as possible, then all the newly freed people could get to the North—maybe even Esther. Addy stood quietly by herself for a minute, her heart aching with the memory of her baby sister. Then she turned and went inside to pick up the scissors.

Addy headed toward Mr. Delmonte's store. It was still open. She could see the pretty red scarf tucked behind the tea kettle in the window. But Addy didn't go inside. Instead, she walked on down the street for a few more blocks until she came to the church. With both hands, she pulled open the heavy door. She walked over to the box at the side of the church. Above it was a sign that said, "Freedmen's Fund." Slowly, Addy took off her mitten. One by one, she dropped her coins into the box. The last coin was the half dime Uncle Solomon had given her. She remembered the words he said to her, "Freedom's got a cost." Then she thought of Esther, Sam, and Poppa, still waiting to take their freedom, and she let the half dime clink into the box with the rest of her money.

☀

Addy was glad to have a job to do. It helped her get her mind off the scarf. But more than anything, she was glad to be with Momma.

C HAPTER
F IVE
—

CHRISTMAS SURPRISES

From that day on, Addy was allowed to spend her afternoons sewing in the warm shop with Momma and Mrs. Ford instead of in the cold garret by herself. Business had begun to slow down. Momma and Mrs. Ford were just finishing up a few small items.

Four days before Christmas, Addy was straightening up the shop for Mrs. Ford. She loved to sort the buttons into boxes, arrange the feathers according to size, and straighten the creamy laces and loopy fringes. She carefully wound the ribbons back on their spools and organized the thread by color. She folded the beautiful fabrics and piled them neatly on the shelves. By the end of the afternoon, all that was left to do was to pick up the pins that had fallen on the floor in the Christmas bustle.

Addy was on her hands and knees filling the pin box when the door burst open and in stormed an angry woman. Right behind her was a tall, plump girl. Addy knew the woman must be Mrs. Howell because she carried the beautiful green plaid dress that Momma had worked so hard on. She thrust it toward Mrs. Ford.

"Look at this dress," she fumed. "Just look at it!"

Mrs. Ford took the dress and held it up in front of her. The seams on the sides were split open, and the threads of the plaid fabric were frayed. The buttons on the back had popped off. The dress looked wrinkled and droopy, as if someone had tossed it in a heap on the floor.

"This dress was made too small," Mrs. Howell raged. "I've never seen such poor work."

Addy looked at Momma, who kept her eyes on the sewing in her lap. Addy could see Momma's lips tighten in anger.

"Stop right there," Mrs. Ford said firmly. "Ruth Walker here is the best seamstress I've ever had working for me. I am sure the dress was not made

"Look at this dress," Mrs. Howell fumed. "Just look at it!"

too small. It was sewn to the exact measurements we took at the fitting last month. Perhaps Isabella has grown some."

Addy looked at Isabella. She stood near the door, looking at her feet. Her round face flushed pink.

Mrs. Ford went on. "If you are unhappy, Mrs. Howell, I will give you a full refund—not because the dress was poorly made, but because you are dissatisfied."

Mrs. Ford opened the drawer where she kept the money. She reached inside and took out a handful of bills, which she quickly counted into Mrs. Howell's hand. "Now good day to you, madam," Mrs. Ford said coldly as she pushed the drawer shut with a bang.

"Good day!" said Mrs. Howell. A blast of cold air blew into the shop as the door slammed behind them.

Mrs. Ford sat back down. As she picked up her sewing, she said, "I can't believe she acted that way. Some people have no idea what the Christmas season is all about."

☀

As Christmas approached, almost no one came into the shop. All of the dresses had been finished. Addy made her last delivery on the day before Christmas, taking a red hat to a lady on Society Hill. When she returned to the shop in the early afternoon, Momma wasn't there.

"She's gone upstairs for a rest. Your mother's worked hard," said Mrs. Ford. "I plan to close the shop early this afternoon and take a rest myself."

Addy started to head upstairs, but Mrs. Ford stopped her. "Before you go, Addy, I have one last package." She handed a parcel wrapped in brown paper to Addy.

"Who is this for?" Addy asked.

"Open it," said Mrs. Ford. "It's for you."

Addy untied the package and could hardly believe what was inside. It was the green plaid dress Momma had made for Isabella Howell! But it looked like new. All the seams were repaired and the buttons had been replaced.

"I want you to have this dress, Addy," said Mrs. Ford. "You've been such a big help to your mother and me this

45

Christmas season. You have worked hard. I've made the dress smaller to fit you. The hem just needs to be cut to the right length. Slip the dress on now and I'll pin it right up before I leave."

Addy didn't know what to say. She just stared at the dress. "Yes, ma'am," she said.

Addy stood on a crate while Mrs. Ford kneeled on the floor, measuring the hem and putting pins in at the right length. Addy turned in a circle, taking tiny steps as the skirt of the dress was marked to the proper length. Then she took off the dress so Mrs. Ford could cut off the extra material.

When Mrs. Ford was finished, the long, wide piece of material she had cut from the bottom of the dress was hanging around her neck. Seeing it gave Addy an idea.

"Mrs. Ford, can I have the material you cut from the dress?" asked Addy.

"Certainly, Addy," replied Mrs. Ford. "All of this dress belongs to you. Now sit right down here and sew up the hem. You know how to do that. I'll be leaving now. But you can stay down here where the light is better and let your mother rest. When you're through, don't forget to put out the lamp."

"Yes, ma'am," said Addy. "And thank you, Mrs. Ford. Thank you for such a beautiful dress."

"You're welcome, Addy," said Mrs. Ford. "Merry Christmas."

❋

On Christmas morning, the sun shone brightly. Addy and Momma woke early, excited to spend their first Christmas in freedom. Momma spoke first. "I know you awake, bright eyes," she said. "Merry Christmas."

"Merry Christmas, Momma," Addy said, sitting up in bed. Sun streamed in the window, and the frosty panes looked as though they were covered with a delicate lace.

"I got a surprise for you, honey," said Momma. She handed Addy a small parcel wrapped in paper.

"I got one for you, too, Momma," said Addy excitedly.

"You open yours first," laughed Momma.

So Addy untied the string. As the paper fell away, she saw a little rag doll with a bright red smile stitched on her face. She had a bow tucked in her hair, tiny

47

hoop earrings, and a purple dress.

Addy beamed with joy. "Momma, she so pretty," she said happily, hugging the doll. "She just as pretty as Janie was."

Momma smiled at Addy. "I stuffed her with some beans I saved."

Addy hugged the doll. The beans gave her a lumpy plumpness that Addy liked. "I'll call her Ida Bean," said Addy with a giggle. "Now, Momma, sit down and hide your eyes while I get my surprise for you. Don't look, because mine ain't wrapped." Addy hopped out of bed and went across the room to her school satchel. She took out the gift she'd hidden inside.

"Are your eyes still closed, Momma?" Addy asked before turning around.

"Sure enough," said Momma.

Addy ran across the floor and placed her gift on Momma's lap.

"Now you can open your eyes," said Addy.

When Momma looked down, there was a lovely scarf of beautiful green plaid before her. The edges were sewn with tiny perfect stitches and the ends were fringed.

"Addy! Where'd you get this?" asked Momma in surprise.

Addy told Momma all about the dress Mrs. Ford had repaired for her and about the extra material that was left when she cut off the bottom to make the dress fit Addy. "I spent yesterday afternoon hemming the dress and making the extra material into a scarf for you, Momma," Addy explained. "Oh, Addy," said Momma gently, running her hands across the plaid. "It's beautiful. Ain't we gonna look fine going to church this evening?" Momma gave Addy a long hug. "I'm proud of my girl!" she said.

Ida Bean sat on Addy's lap while she and Momma had breakfast together. Then Addy put on her apron and propped Ida Bean in a chair so she could watch as Addy and Momma made sweet-potato pudding. There was some pudding left over, so Momma put it in a small pan.

"We can leave this one here and have it tomorrow," Momma said.

By the middle of the afternoon, the pudding was done, and its sweet spicy smell filled the tiny garret. Then Momma and Addy got ready for church. Addy wore her beautiful new dress, and Momma took time braiding and fixing Addy's hair. Momma put her new scarf around her neck and tied it in a big bow. Addy thought Momma had never looked more beautiful.

"I'm gonna take Ida Bean with me to show Sarah," said Addy, tucking her doll under her arm. Then Addy and Momma headed down the stairs and out to church.

As they got closer to church, the sun was setting. They could hear the organ music. When they opened the big doors to the church and stepped inside, Addy knew that Sarah had been right. The altar *did* look magical, with the manger scene and the silvery star shining high above.

Addy and Momma had just been seated when a loud chord blasted from the organ. The choir began to walk down the aisle singing "Joy to the World" in strong, happy voices. A glow filled the dark church as the choir marched in. Each member held a candle that cast shadows into the church. Addy watched for Sarah, who was at the front of the choir. Sarah turned and smiled at Addy. Addy gave a shy wave back. She felt tears run down her cheeks. She was crying because the church was so beautiful and the choir sounded so good and she and Momma were together.

When the service was over, everyone went down to Fellowship Hall for dinner. There was turkey and dressing, squash and greens, cornbread and applesauce. Addy had never had so much food on her plate at one time. When it was time to go back for dessert, Addy ignored all the cakes and pies and headed straight for Momma's sweet-potato pudding in the shining black skillet. As she savored each smooth sweet bite, she thought about Poppa, Sam, and Esther. *Maybe next Christmas,* she thought. *Maybe next Christmas we'll all be together, eating Momma's sweet-potato pudding.*

After dinner, the adults lingered over their coffee while the children hurried to the room set up for the shadow play. Sarah and Addy sat on a bench next to each other with Ida Bean snuggled between them. When all the children were settled, the door was closed. The lamps on the walls were blown out and the room was completely dark. The children squealed with excitement and pretended to be scared. After a minute, a lamp began to glow behind the sheet in front of the room. All eyes watched as the first shadow figure appeared on the sheet and the Christmas story was read aloud.

One figure and then another and another appeared on the sheet until soon Addy could see the shadow of Mary bent over the manger, holding her newborn baby, with Joseph standing at her side. Three shepherds stood beside them. A deep, rolling voice continued to read as all the children sat in the dark, quietly watching the shapes against the lighted sheet.

As the star appeared to guide the wise men, the door at the side of the room opened. A shaft of light from the hall filled the darkened room. The children turned to see who had opened the door. It was a tall man. Though Addy could not see his face, his shadow was a shape she recognized. Addy jumped up and struggled through the rows of children, tripping over their feet, stumbling as she hurried to the door. Addy knew who was standing in the door, standing there right now, not in a dream, not someday, but right now.

"Poppa," she burst out. "Poppa, is that you?"

"Is that my Addy?" came the answer.

It was Poppa! Addy rushed to him and he swept her up into his strong arms and held her close for a long time.

☀

It was dark by the time Addy, Poppa, and Momma headed back to the garret, walking hand in hand through the Christmas streets. When they got to the top of the stairs above Mrs. Ford's shop, Addy could see light under their door.

"That's strange," Momma said. "We didn't leave the candle burning."

back with us so we can all be together right here in Philadelphia like we planned. There was a freedmen's society in Maryland that helped me come here to you. Maybe the freedmen's society in Philadelphia can help us."

Addy laid her head against Poppa's chest. She felt certain that their dream would happen. "One day," she said, "we all gonna be together—all of us with Esther and Sam, too."

"You tired, Addy," Momma said. "It's time you got ready for bed."

"Can't I stay up longer?" Addy asked.

"You want to sit up all night like a little ol' owl?" Poppa teased.

Addy laughed. "Yes, Poppa. I want to stay up and be with you."

"Well, I ain't going nowhere. I'm gonna be here when you wake up in the morning," Poppa said. "I'll be the first thing you see when the sun comes in that window."

"Addy loved that window from the second we moved in here," Momma said, "but it got stuck about a month ago and we can't get it down."

"Let me have a look at it," Poppa said. He lifted

Addy off his lap and went over to the window. Momma and Addy followed him. Poppa studied the window and then hit the frame in two places. Then he pulled down hard and closed the window.

"There!" said Poppa. "It needs a new sash. I can make that. But it should be warmer in here now."

"It already is," said Addy. She and Momma put their arms around Poppa. In the window, Addy could see their happy faces reflected in the glow of the lamplight.

**LOOKING
BACK
1864**

A Peek Into
the Past

A mess hall for Union soldiers, decorated with holiday evergreens.

Christmas was a difficult time for people during the Civil War. Many families worried about loved ones fighting in the war. Many had lost sons, husbands, or fathers in the war. Some families, like Addy's, had been separated by slavery. In northern cities, churches and other organizations helped some people, like Poppa, get to the North and find their families. But many people who had been enslaved were never able to find their relatives.

Most families, black or white, in the North or South, celebrated Christmas in some small way during the Civil

Children at the time of the Civil War.

War. Holiday foods and gifts had to be simple because prices had gone up during the war. People who had recently escaped slavery usually had little extra money to spend on holidays. But even poor parents like Addy's mother

A handmade toy.

tried to make Christmas special for their children. They might have made a festive meal and given each child a homemade or inexpensive gift.

In many parts of the South, food became scarce as the war went on, making it hard to cook holiday meals. People in some areas didn't have enough food and suffered from hunger. They learned to use substitutes for things they couldn't get, like using ground chestnuts to make coffee. Cookbooks even told women how to make apple pie without apples!

This book of "receipts," or recipes, helped people cook despite shortages caused by the Civil War.

Life was not as hard in most parts of the North. Families that had a little spare money decorated their homes with evergreens and put up a Christmas tree.

Charlotte Forten.

Charlotte Forten, a young African-American woman who taught freed slaves in South Carolina during the war, wrote in her diary about a Christmas visit to friends in Philadelphia in 1864. She enjoyed watching the adults give their children gifts, and in the evening there was a special meal, followed by games and singing.

Many northern and southern women raised money for a special Christmas meal for wounded soldiers in nearby hospitals. During the last years of the war, when black men from the North became soldiers, women at Philadelphia's Mother Bethel African Methodist Episcopal Church held holiday fairs to raise money for the soldiers. Addy attended a church like Mother Bethel and might have helped with such a fair.

Soldiers in Civil War camps rarely had much of a Christmas celebration. Many prayed and sang patriotic or Christmas songs, remembering

Photos of family members were treasured by soldiers fighting in the war.

62

their families and better times. The officers of one regiment treated their men to apple dumplings on

Christmas Day. Some lucky soldiers received boxes filled with food treats from their families. Some might have received a pair of handmade socks—a welcome gift for soldiers who often had no warm clothes. But many families did not know where their soldiers were and could not send holiday remembrances.

Soldiers around a fire.

Enslaved people celebrated Christmas before and during the war, too. Most slave owners gave slaves three to six days off from work at Christmastime. On Christmas morning at many plantations, slaves gathered at their owner's home to receive small gifts like ribbons, handkerchiefs, and coins. Owners often gave out extra meat, tobacco, and molasses then, too. Most important, slaves were usually allowed to visit their relatives and friends on neighboring farms or in town for festive celebrations.

At these gatherings, enslaved children

An African-American fiddle player.

63

ran races, played games, and told ghost stories. It was popular in southern states for young men to shoot guns on Christmas morning. Since slaves couldn't own guns, slave children sometimes made their own "Christmas guns." They cleaned hog bladders after butchering time, blew them up, tied them closed, and let them dry. On Christmas morning, they held them on sticks over a fire until they exploded.

The last day of the Christmas holiday was sometimes called "heartbreak day" because of the great sadness of leaving relatives and friends once the holiday was over.

An event that took place on January 1, 1863, made New Year's Day an especially meaningful holiday for African Americans. On that day, President Abraham Lincoln issued his Emancipation Proclamation, which freed slaves in most parts of the South. Although the South ignored the Proclamation, it did make slaves and abolitionists feel hopeful that slavery would end. In many northern cities that year, blacks and whites gathered in churches on New Year's Eve for special

President Lincoln and his Emancipation Proclamation.

"Emancipation-watch" services. The Proclamation was read just after midnight, followed by joyful songs and prayers. Men shouted, women fainted, whites and blacks shook hands, and cannons were fired when the Proclamation was read aloud. Emancipation celebrations continue to be held on New Year's Day in many areas of the North and South. People in some parts of the country celebrate other days when slaves first learned about the Proclamation, such as June 19, or *Juneteenth*.

A new festival, Kwanzaa, has also become important in recent years. Kwanzaa was created in 1966 to honor the African heritage of black Americans. It begins on December 26 and ends on New Year's Day, the same day as the anniversary of the Emancipation Proclamation. Festivities include singing, a feast, the exchange of small gifts, and decorating homes with an African theme. In Addy's day and in ours, holiday celebrations like Christmas, Emancipation Day, and Kwanzaa are important times for loved ones to be together.

The Kwanzaa candleholder represents the people and cultures of Africa.